Sister Trees

ISBN 978-1-0980-9166-8 (paperback)
ISBN 978-1-63874-266-1 (hardcover)
ISBN 978-1-0980-9167-5 (digital)

Christian Faith Publishing, Inc.
832 Park Avenue
Meadville, PA 16335
www.christianfaithpublishing.com

Printed in the United States of America

Sister Trees

Stephanie Ferguson

Sister trees are rooted in the grassy field,
standing tall and strong.

Colossians 2:7

As the sun rises above the horizon, sister trees wake together
to the chirping song of the birds resting in their branches.

Psalm 113:3

Soaking up the sun's rays, the sister trees
glow and smile from the warmth.

Malachi 4:2

Dancing green leaves twist and shimmer as the sister friends sway in the gentle breeze.

Amos 4:13

Bird families nest in the safety of the sister trees'
strong arms, singing songs of happiness.

Psalm 84:3

New life emerges from the speckled eggs that shiver
and crack, filling the sisters' hearts with joy.

Jeremiah 1:5

Little brown squirrels play among the sister trees'
limbs. They chase, hide, and leap from tree to tree.
The sister trees giggle together at the tickle of the
little squirrel feet scampering upon their arms.

Genesis 1:25

Black crows swoop into the trees, perching on
branches. They caw to one another as they nestle in
the camouflage of the sister trees' soft leaves.

Luke 12:24

As the sky turns dark, the sisters hug each other. They huddle together and summon their courage as the storm swirls around them.

Isaiah 4:6

Sister trees are not frightened, for they are rooted and grounded in the earth. Their leaves rustle in the rising wind while the rain pelts their leaves, limbs, and trunks. The sisters hold hands and laugh with delight as the rain washes them clean.

John 14:27

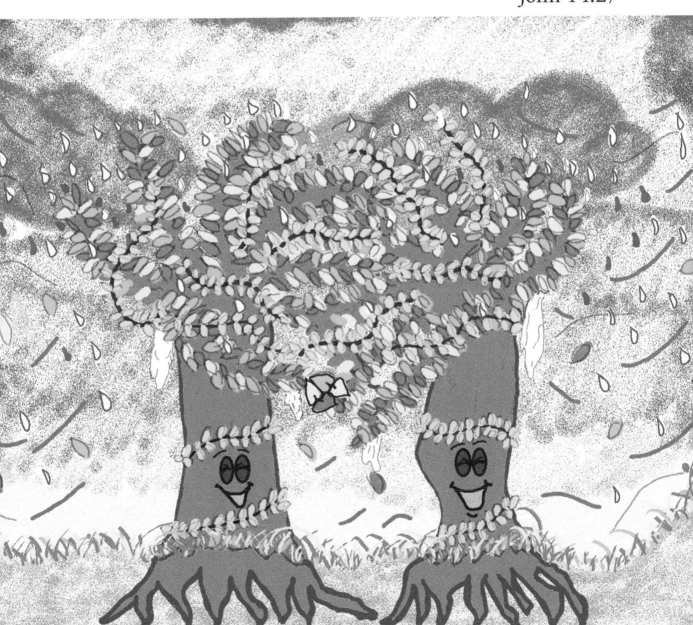

Inhaling the clean air after the storm passes, the
sisters are strengthened by their courage, faith,
and the fresh scent of the rain-cooled air.

1 Corinthians 16:13

Sister trees lounge and laze in the rays of sun peeking through the disappearing clouds. The colors of the rainbow kiss their leaves, reminding them of the truth of God's promises.

Genesis 9:13

The moon rises in the sky while the sisters happily
dance together to the hum of the frogs and cicadas.

Psalm 42:8

Two fearless sister trees drift into a peaceful sleep.
They rest to get ready for another beautiful day.

Psalm 4:8

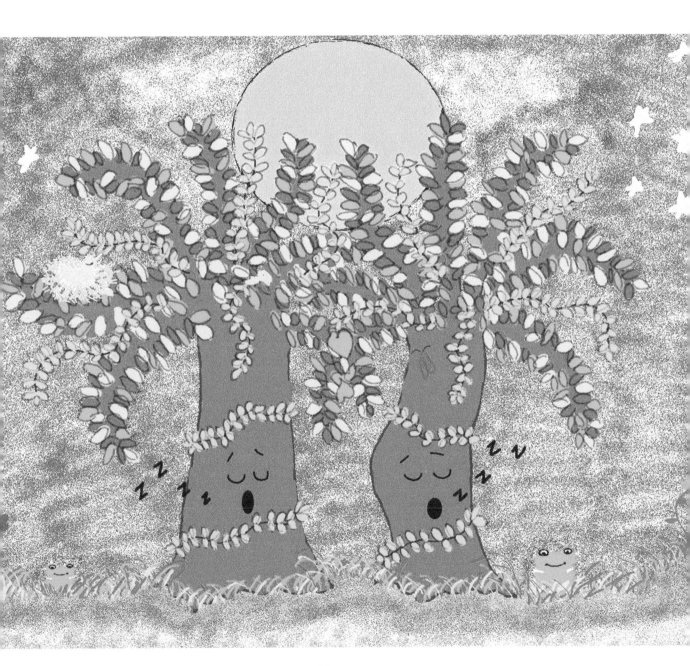

About the Author

Stephanie Ferguson earned a bachelor's degree in education from East Central University. She spent nineteen years teaching young children in the public school system. Today she still enjoys reading books to children as a librarian. Stephanie and her husband have one grown son, and they live in Southern Oklahoma.